LISTENING TO JAZZ,

AND FALLING IN LOVE:

Two of Life's Most Enjoyable
Experiences Especially on a Cruise

WALLACE S. HALL

ISBN
978-1-957378-14-5 (Paperback)
978-1-957378-13-8 (eBook)

TABLE OF CONTENTS

CHAPTER ONE

"JEAN IS DEAD, MAN." Raymond Johnson said to his best friend, Walter Henderson, over the phone. Crying disrupted his speech. Jean had died in November 2014, from an aggressive liver cancer.

"Aw man, I know how much you meant to each other. The Lord works in mysterious ways."

Walter, since his fourth marriage fifteen years earlier, had become devoutly religious. Raymond is an agnostic; he and Jean had been married for over 60 years.

Raymond and Walter had lived comfortable lives for decades; both were successful, minority entrepreneurs. They were so close they could finish each other's sentences, always with a laugh. At age eighty-six, Raymond was five years Walter's senior; they had been best friends for fifty years. Various religious beliefs were insignificant.

"What can I do to help, my brother?" Asked Walter.

Jean's passing was devastating to Raymond. The thought of living alone frightened him; initially he did not know if he would make it. The foursome's lives, including Nancy, Walter wife, had been intertwined for decades. Both couples had lived in St. Louis earlier.

Jean's cremation occurred in Atlanta, where Jean, Raymond and Leona had lived for over fifteen years. Leona, Jean and Raymond's oldest of three children, still lived there. Walter and Nancy attended her cremation ceremony, but Raymond did not. The emotional stress might have been detrimental, counseled Raymond's doctor, considering Raymond's heart surgery several years earlier. Leona had been a single mom and Jean and Raymond had helped raise her two sons while she traveled on business extensively.

Decades earlier, Walter had joked more than once while having drinks amongst friends in their favorite St. Louis bar, where Walter was the wealthy neighborhood raconteur. When asked by a newbie, if he and Raymond were brothers; he answered, "No; but we're about the same ugly." Both were similar statured with light skin coloring, around six feet, and nice looking African American men.

When they lived in St. Louis, hardly a day passed without Walter and Raymond talking. Walter now lived in Richmond Heights, Arkansas, with his fourth wife Nancy. Raymond had been the Best Man and Jean the Maid of Honor, at their wedding in St. Thomas, seventeen years prior, while enjoying a jazz cruise.

Raymond and Jean had moved to Colorado Springs about twenty years earlier. The foursome had communicated regularly, and enjoyed cruises together. They shared significant, celebratory occasions over the years.

"I'm going to come out to Colorado Springs and spend a week or two, to help you get through your tragedy by our praying together, my brother."

"Aw man, thanks a lot but that won't be necessary; I'll get through it, one way or another. I appreciate the thought, but it will be forever before I am back to normal."

"Okay, then I'll call you every Tuesday and Thursday before noon, and you better answer the phone, or I'll be knocking on your door."

"I can handle that."

And so it was, Walter and Raymond communicated regularly, for at least a half-hour, twice weekly, for months; reliving and sometimes exaggerating memories while sharing deep laughs. It was great therapy for Raymond.

During the winter of 2015, Walter suggested, "Why don't you come out here and spend a week next summer?"

Nancy's large family were founders of their church; she sang in the choir, and was a devout Baptist. Sunday services, Wednesday choir practice, and Thursday's Bible study, were intricate parts of her week. When everyone attended, the congregation was fifty strong, including children.

Walter had discarded his raucous past that he and Raymond had shared, because of Nancy's religious lifestyle. Walter became the teacher of the Sunday school Bible class, and had become a true believer; he constantly read the Bible; he swore that he had experienced several miracles. Because of his business acumen, he was an asset on the church's board.

Richmond Heights' population was twenty thousand. Their most popular, social location was the restaurant in Wal-Mart. Everybody in town knew Nancy; she worked in the County Tax Collector's office. Nancy's four sisters, after learning Raymond was in town, about his recent loss, and knowing he had a "sweet tooth", flooded Nancy's kitchen with homemade desserts. Raymond picked up ten pounds in a week.

One day after dinner, Nancy suggested, "I know you miss Jean, as we all do, but you still have a life to live, Raymond; why don't you and Walter take a jazz cruise, with the hope of your meeting somebody? I'm sure Jean wouldn't want you to spend the rest of your life alone."

"You're right, I do miss Jean. It is impossible to overstate the happiness we shared. Raising our children was a joy. Our happiness was continuous. We never had a serious disagreement. Oh, I played poker a little too much, but it never affected our lifestyle. After twenty years, we could anticipate each other's thoughts; after fifty years, we communicated with just a smile. We were very fortunate to have friends like you. Taking a cruise is a great suggestion, Nancy. Hey buddy, ready for another cruise?" asked Raymond.

"Sounds good to me," said Walter. "I know you love jazz more than me. You have said earlier, one can hear a fifty-year-old Coleman Hawkins number and it will sound as contemporary as something that was recorded last month. In addition, you and I agree, the music heard on cruises is entirely different from what is played in clubs, or on records. I have not been on a jazz cruise since our last one over ten years ago. What would you do darling, without me being here?" Walter asked Nancy.

"I could use the rest."

Raymond and Walter booked space on the next available jazz cruise, sailing in February 2017; the 'All That Jazz Cruise'.

*   *   *

"I'm not taking you on the cruise with me this year, Agnes," Loretta, her sixty-year-old, sister scolded. "You were just too forward last time."

Both women had been married and divorced; Loretta twice. Neither had had any children. Agnes had been a teacher for thirty years. Loretta, who had earned a Master of Psychology Degree, was a human research executive with a major company; she was upper-middle class. They lived together in Tucson, Arizona. They both attended church services regularly, but Loretta was more religious, and self-disciplined.

Loretta and Agnes took several trips a year to jazz festivals, some, where they stayed overnight, but Loretta had decided she would enjoy the jazz cruise more if she didn't have to worry about the shapelier, fun-loving, adventuresome, Agnes' loose virtues, even at fifty.

"That's entirely up to you darling sister; I can take it or leave it. Just because you changed your lifestyle, and never bothered to change back after two failed marriages, doesn't mean shit to me; I still get satisfaction from a handsome, well-hung, dude. However, I will miss the music. I'll just have to find something to do while you're gone." A wicked smile parted her lips, with glistening eyes..

Loretta, five foot seven, full figured, attractive, and African American, booked her single passage on the All That Jazz Cruise, sailing from Miami February 2017, nine months away.

CHAPTER TWO

THE SAILING DATE FINALLY arrived. Raymond and Walter met in the Miami Airport, and took a cab to the loading dock. After checking in with passports, their luggage was taken to their designated level by a large crane, and was then moved to their cabin by the ship's casual labor.

Walter and Raymond followed the suggestion of a ship's steward, and went to the twelfth level where food and drinks were available in a massive cafeteria. As they enjoyed a delicious snack, they faintly heard some swinging music. After eating, they followed the rhythmic sounds, which led them to the rear deck.

Approximately forty passengers were doing "The Electric Slide." It was a 'community' dance. The 'Slide's music was not even close to jazz, but nobody cared. Four swinging lines were enjoying the semi-complicated, multi-stepping, dance. The ship's D.J. certainly knew how to make jazz cruise passengers feel welcome on their first day.

Ladies, dressed from the ridiculous to the sublime, were shaking their "tail feathers", men were stepping in time, while bending their upper torsos, The "Electric Slide" had become the most popular group dance amongst African Americans in years. Walter and Raymond danced as long as they could; about fifteen minutes, and then returned to the cafeteria.

A couple was sitting at a table for four. "May we join you?" Walter asked.

The woman smiled, "Of course you can. Meeting new people is one of the many advantages of taking a cruise, I'm Camellia, and this is my husband, Howard."

Howard added, "We're from Detroit, and take cruises quarterly. Of course, none are as enjoyable as this one!"

"He's Walter, from Richmond Heights, Arkansas, and I'm Raymond from Colorado Springs. We have taken many jazz cruises previously, but not recently, and none with this cruise line." A waiter took Walter and Raymond's drink order.

As the foursome talked about everyone's favorite subject, jazz, Walter noticed an attractive woman sitting by herself at the nearby, curved bar. She looked very independent. Walter subtly alerted Raymond to her presence. For about fifteen minutes, Raymond attempted eye contact but was unsuccessful.

Walter whispered, "You have to do or say something, man. You just cannot let her sit there. Sooner or later, somebody is going to engage her, and you will be crying in your soup for the rest of the cruise."

"She might be waiting on her man, man," Raymond responded.

"Then again, she may not. You have to find out! What have you got to lose?"

Raymond sauntered over. "That's a mighty large bottle of water you're drinking from, Missy; are they available on ship?" It was a quart-size bottle. *That was safe; at least she cannot accuse me of harassing her,* decided Raymond.

"No it's not. I bought a case on board, so I would not have to buy pints of water at exorbitant prices. If you like, I will bring you and your friend a bottle. Incidentally, how did you know my name was Missy?" She said smiling.

Raymond internally evaluated her response. *That was friendly. She could have answered the question with a callous, "No". Her challenging the word Missy left an opening. She is probably a strange bird; how can you carry a case of water on a cruise ship because you are concerned about the price?*

"I had the option of ending my intrusive remark by addressing you as 'Girl', 'Woman', 'Lady', 'Ma'am', 'Madam', Miss, Golden Ager, Senior Citizen, or 'Missy'. Most of those names seemed inappropriate, especially the last two. I thought 'Missy' was the friendlier, and a more personal term, which is usually used when addressing young, attractive, women." Raymond changed the subject. "That is very thoughtful of you, to share your water reserves. May I buy you a cocktail in response to your generosity and sensitivity? Incidentally, are you traveling alone?"

"Yes, I am."

"Well, one of the many advantages of taking a cruise is meeting new people," Raymond said, repeating Camellia's welcoming remark. "Why don't you join us? We were strangers just moments ago, now we are fast friends."

"I'd like that, but my name is Loretta, not Missy."

"Okay, okay." Raymond hurriedly moved an empty table next to their table of four, moved his seat to the new table, and put a chair beside his, for Loretta.

"We're from Detroit, Michigan, and take cruises quarterly," Camellia said.

"I'm from Tucson, Arizona. This is my fourth jazz cruise with this company. I enjoy the music and the comradery. I have met several of the musicians, and become friends with many of the repeat passengers."

Raymond and Loretta talked amongst themselves. Raymond learned about Loretta's career, her jazz interests, and that she sang in her church choir. She was obviously middle-class, and Raymond diplomatically avoided the question of age; he surmised she was in her fifties.

It was almost four-thirty. The day had passed rapidly; it was time to set sail.

"This is the First Mate speaking. May I have your attention please," came over the ship's speaker system. "Before setting sail, we are required to assign each passenger to a lifeboat, in case of an emergency. Your cabin numbers will correlate with your lifeboat's location. Please proceed to the exit nearest you; one of the ship's crewmembers will direct you further, once you reveal your cabin number. Thank you."

As soon as Loretta and Raymond exited the cafeteria, they were separated based upon their cabin numbers. Each was directed toward their lifeboat position. After the drill, Raymond returned to the cafeteria, but Loretta was not there. He and Walter went to their cabin, refreshed themselves, and dressed in coats, sports shirts, and slacks, for dinner. Not wearing coats while having dinner was acceptable, but Walter and Raymond had been concerned about their appearance all of their lives. After dinner, Walter and Raymond went back to the cafeteria, and was disappointed a second time.

While sitting in a lounge, Walter said, "Obviously you are impressed with Loretta. However, you have no idea how many 'lonely and alone foxes' there are on this ship. Why don't you give yourself a chance to see what's available before you make a commitment?"

"Loretta and I spent three hours together; that was enough time for me to realize I am very attracted to her, potentially beyond this cruise. I hope the feeling was mutual."

After a half-hour in the lounge, Walter said, "My hip is bothering me. I have done a lot of walking today; I am going to take it easy and return to our cabin."

"But they have Count Basie's orchestra playing tonight."

"Count Basie died over thirty years ago," said Walter.

"I know that, but several bands have been sustained after the death of their leader. Their bandsmen have arranged with their heirs and continued the musical legends. Duke Ellington's band is managed by his son, Mercer."

"Listen man, you go ahead; I need the rest."

As Raymond walked toward the twin-deck auditorium, he encountered Camellia and Howard. "Hey people, you going to hear Count?"

"That's the plan, it's amazing. It will probably be a trip back into the forties and fifties, when big bands flourished. Of course I'm sure they will have a few new arrangements."

"Scotty Barnhart is now the manager and bandleader. They hired a new pianist who made a career of sounding like the Count, named Julius Marshall, " said Raymond.

"You sound like a jazz musician; otherwise how would you know who is leading the Count Basie Band, or playing Count-like piano?"

"I'm not a musician but I am a jazz historian. I have been following jazz for over seventy years. I played the trombone when I was in high school, but it did not work out. I am sure you remember, 'Mr. Five by Five', Jimmy Rushing, and Joe Williams, as featured singers with the Count; but you probably do not remember that Billie Holliday also sang with Count's orchestra. Trumpeter, Harry 'Sweets' Edison, and Lester 'Prez' Young, played with the Count, back in 'the day'."

"Damn, man, you sure have a deep memory bank."

"It is not all memory. I am a writer and research most questions that come to mind. Who knows, one day I might write a book about jazz."

"You know you have just obligated yourself," said Camellia.

"How?"

"Any question I have about jazz, I'll ask you."

"No problem. If I don't have the answer, I'll look it up on Wikipedia."

The performance was outstanding. They started with "One O'clock Jump". Not only did Scotty Barnhart play most of Count Basie's standards, he also had singers who sang songs that Joe Williams, Jimmy Rushing, and Billie Holliday had made famous. They also played some new, beautiful, arrangements of standards, like "Somewhere over the Rainbow", and "Stardust."

The orchestra completed their performance with Count's signature number, "April in Paris". The number was closing down with a brass-bellowing, six-bar finish, with Count Basie's voice saying "One more time," then the orchestra repeated the six-bar refrain, only louder and higher, in another key, with the Count's voice closing out the number saying the immortal and unique, "One more once". It was a fabulous opening evening for a jazz cruise. The Count Basie Orchestra would play "under the stars" Wednesday night, encouraging the passengers to dance. .

After the concert, Raymond toured the ship looking for Loretta. He visited the Meet and Greet Singles Lounge, where there were several attractive women, but Raymond did not engage them in casual conversations on the chance that Loretta would appear, and consider him nothing more than a flirt. He also visited the twin bars on the ninth level, where dancing prevailed. Raymond took a seat at the bar, ordered a drink, and watched women dancing with each other, "silently begging" for a man to inject himself, but Raymond did not dance; he was waiting, and looking, for Loretta.

The activities ended around eleven thirty. Raymond stopped in another lounge and listened to musicians jam, but only for a half-hour, hoping that Loretta might appear; she did not. He finally went to bed around midnight.

CHAPTER THREE

WALTER AND RAYMOND AWAKENED with the sun; they were in the twenty-four-hour cafeteria having coffee at six, with additional early risers. Bland conversations occurred. No one wanted to talk seriously; they were on vacation. After trading names, hometowns, hobbies, and how often one cruised, the conversations usually turned to everyone's common interest: jazz and musicians they had discovered, who were still unknown.

Howard had an expensive camera that Walter admired; Raymond had a hardbound twelve by fifteen book of jazz performers' photographs, and appropriate prose from the fifties that his late wife had given him over twenty years ago. Many stars had autographed their photos. Camellia enjoyed reviewing the photographs; some were acquaintances.

"We should have done something like this," Camellia said to Howard. She made remarks regarding musicians in Raymond's book with which she and Howard had had encounters. Raymond felt good about having bought along his cherished gift.

Everyone had an iPhone. Between conversation contributions, everyone was 'working' his or her phone. Raymond's heart skipped a beat: in walked Loretta, "Well, hello there," he said as calmly as he could.

"I tried to find your cabin number but all I had was your first names," Loretta said. "I thought I would find you two here."

"I had the same problem," Raymond said. He could not stop smiling. Not only was he pleased to see Loretta; he learned she had tried to find him, which meant she was interested. *Of course, she did not have to mention Walter,* Raymond thought.

The five of them moved to a larger table. Raymond immediately wrote down Loretta's cabin and phone number and gave her his.

Loretta said hello to musicians and friends from previous cruises who passed by their table. Occasionally, she introduced her new friends. Together, the group enjoyed their first morning at sea.

It was Sunday morning. The first planned event was a gospel, soul-stirring presentation at ten o'clock. They would perform in the ship's main, two tier, thousand-seat auditorium. The ship's musical director had invited, gratuitously twenty-five singers, and their director. The instrumentalists were the ship's sidemen, a pianist, a drummer, and a guitarist. *That is the pianist I heard last night,* thought Raymond.

The singers were outstanding, they vocalized in perfect harmony. Their complicated arrangements were unusually beautiful; altos, tenors, sopranos, and bassists, sang separately, then together. Two women and one man performed stirring solos; all three felt 'the Spirit,' and had to be "supported" by fellow choir members just before completing their performances. The audience, which half-filled the theater, enjoyed their soulful presentations.

The choir was dressed in yellow robes with billowing sleeves and white piping. They were standing on a three-level portable, platform. The men wore white shirts with yellow ties under their robes; the women wore white blouses. Their director led them, mouthing the lyrics, with a rhythmic sway that included in-time stepping, shoulder shuffling, head moves, and synchronized arm motions. The songs were spiritually stimulating.

Their audience listened as they clapped singularly, waved, stood, lifting their arms with open hands, shouting, "Amen," and, "God is good; all the time." The performance was moving, even for a non-believer like Raymond. "The Spirit" overtook several women in the audience; they were "assisted" by men wearing white suits and gloves. Raymond believed the "overtaken" women were part of the entertainment. The musical spiritual lasted an hour.

The African American, Detroit church choir recorded their songs; they had planned to sell their presentation on board, as well as when they returned home, as a fundraiser. The Musical Cruise Director had the ability to produce CD's for sale.

After the gospel singing, Loretta and Raymond sat alone, together, on the pool deck in comfortable lounges, in the shade, refreshed by tropical breezes, and umbrella-decorated drinks as their ship parted the ocean's smooth waters while creating small, white capped waves.

"So," Raymond asked, "What interests you?"

"Obviously I enjoy jazz. As I said earlier. I am also a devout Methodist; I spend most of Sunday in church; praying, counseling, and singing. I like to read Christian books, novels, and the Bible. Where do your interests lie?"

I really like this woman and there is no benefit in me telling her I am an Agnostic. I am not sure of her commitment; many people say they are religious, but only practice what is compatible. Some treat religion as a social experience rather than a lifestyle. "Well, I'm a non-practicing Catholic, a widower, a writer, and like you, a jazz devotee, I have been retired for almost twenty years, and am presently alone and very lonely. I also spend quite a bit of time researching, mostly the Black community." *That was safe.*

"What have you learned?"

"That African Americans are headed in the right direction."

"Elaborate, please."

"This is just one statistic; half of all advanced degrees are earned by Blacks under the age of twenty five.

"Why is that significant?"

"We only represent seventeen percent of the Nation's population, yet Caucasians only achieve fifteen percent of the advanced degrees; WE receive over fifty percent. To me it means that African Americans, generally, understand that the pathway to equality and monetary success is through Education. Of course, equality is not guaranteed by higher education. Those who determine our level of responsibility, our income, and our promotions, are ultimately, and individually, responsible for our equality, and are mostly White. You have obviously learned this fact; you have a Masters in Social Studies, and work for an international company, responsible for International Human Relations. An equality-minded, executive made that decision in your behalf. But we still have a long way to go for most of US to reach equality."

"What do you mean?"

For every one thousand dollars in equity WE poses, Caucasians have ten thousand. Equality will be when both races' financial equity is similar. Over the last hundred years,

Caucasians, with the support of Government, have illegally robbed US of our land and business. Illegal assassinations, destroying our profitable businesses, and taking our Real Estate has happened all over the country. Tulsa Oklahoma is just one example."

I am impressed; thought Loretta, *Raymond is a deep thinker.* "Have you taken this cruise before?" asked Loretta, changing the conversation to less technical matters.

"No, this is my first cruise with this company. It has been a while since I have been on a jazz cruise. I have sailed on the BOSS Jazz Cruises several times, on Norwegian ships. Since you are familiar with the musicians, the ship, and are travelling alone, perhaps you can be Walter's and my guide this week."

"I'd like that," Loretta answered. She opened her ship's brochure/agenda, and then said, "After lunch there is a performance I think you will enjoy."

"Say no more. If you think it's worth seeing, we'll see it; how's that?"

Loretta smiled, and Raymond smiled back. They had established a platonic relationship. Loretta and Raymond had lunch on the pool deck. Hamburgers, French fries, Polish sausages, chili, salads, and condiments, was the selection. Their selected performance was a half-hour away.

Raymond called Walter on the ship's phone, "We're on our way to the Constellation Lounge on the rear of Level Nine to hear someone Loretta thinks is great, at two."

"Not that you care, but I'll meet you there," Walter answered.

The room accommodated a hundred people on elevated, seats.

Several electricians were ensuring all the microphones, lights, and, electrical instruments were working. Before the performer appeared, audience members publicly asked jazz-oriented questions of fellows .

"Who was the first tenor saxophonist to play smooth jazz that preceded Lester Young?" Raymond asked loudly. The question bounced around the room for several minutes with incorrect names offered.

Finally, a young man answered impatiently, "Why, Coleman Hawkins, people, what kind of jazz fans are you folks?" as if qualifications for being on the cruise included having an extensive, historical, jazz recall.

"Young people are so critical," Raymond said to Loretta.

"Who was the pianist with the first JATP (Jazz at the Philharmonic) group in the fifties?" someone asked; no one answered.

"Nat King Cole, under an assumed name because of his contract with Capitol Records," a mid-sixties passenger correctly answered. "The reason I know is Nat 'King' Cole's name appears on the CD."

"OK, try this on for size," said a senior man from Chicago, "Why was the Nat King Cole trio, a trio?" Silence prevailed. "Because Nat fired his drummer for missing a gig," he answered laughing. "Nat, because he was the group's leader, got twenty dollars. Everyone else received ten dollars for a three-hour gig. After a few successful gigs without a drummer, Nat decided he could work for less, pay his musicians more, and get more gigs. One night, Nat sang while playing, the owner insisted he only play the piano."

Who participated in the greatest jam session ever?" asked a middle-aged, Black woman. Again, silence. The woman answered. "Billie Holliday singing, "My Man don't love me", with Lester Young, Coleman Hawkins, Jerry Mulligan, Ben Webster, Roy Eldridge, and Max Roach, amongst others, playing solos between her unique phrasing. It was a spontaneous happening in a small, crowded, New York studio; fortunately, it was recorded, the year was 1942. Lady Day died in '44.'"

"What instruments did those people you named play, and who was Lady Day?" a young, White man asked.

"If you have to ask, you shouldn't even be on this cruise," answered the woman; the audience said a collective 'amen'.

Rodin Millsap, the performer, was a multiple instrument, blind, musician. As his handler brought him on stage, the audience applauded. A guitar hung over his upper body, with a harmonica against his throat, and a saxophone adjacent to the guitar. Bongos were attached to his waist. Rodin's handler put Rodin's hand on the piano's keys, and told him where the rest of his instruments were. Rodin touched each one. He played eight instruments during his performance; sometimes four during one number. He created the sound of a trumpet with only his mouth and fingers, and sang like Al Hibbler. He changed 'horns' without ever missing a beat. At times, he played two musical instruments concurrently.

Rodin's performance was unique. By closing one's eyes, one could easily believe he/she was listening to at least a quartet. He played all his instruments during his final number, including his "trumpet".

Between numbers, Rodin joked: "Looks as if I have stumbled into a Fifth Avenue boutique, based on how well you people are dressed." That was funny. Nothing could have been further from the truth. Everyone was dressed very casually. His audience wondered how he knew what they were wearing. Rodin "dramatically" "looked" into the first row, stepped off the stage, felt an attractive woman's arm, who was alone, until he reached her hand, kissed the back of her hand, put it in both of his, and said, "Hey baby, I've got my eye on you; you sure are looking good!" The attractive, young, woman blushed. The audience was stunned.

When his performance ended, he received a standing ovation. His handler told him how enthusiastically the audience had responded: he had given Rodin the parameters necessary for him to approach the woman who was sitting alone, and had mentioned the casualness of his audience's attire, before he left the stage.

"I have never heard, or seen, anything like him," was Raymond's post performance comment. He promised himself to buy at least one of Rodin's CDs before leaving the ship.

That evening Loretta treated Raymond and Walter, along with a couple she had known from a previous cruise, to dinner in an excellent, over-staffed, Japanese restaurant. Every diner's water glass was refilled instantly after a sip. It was one of the ship's three fine dining rooms. Raymond was encouraged. He was thoroughly impressed with Loretta and decided to become more verbally intimate.

After dinner, when they were once again alone, Raymond said, "My sex life has been singular since my heart surgery in 1999. The heart specialist ran a catheter from my heart to my genitals during a pre-operational examination. Since the surgery, I have not been able to sustain an erection. I thought it was malpractice. I contacted other urologists but couldn't find one that would sue my heart specialist." Raymond was being completely honest, and very personal. He was interested in establishing a lasting relationship with Loretta that would outlast the cruise.

"That's been almost twenty years. So how have you been satisfying yourself?' Loretta asked.

"Through masturbation," Raymond answered. Silence prevailed. Long moments later, their conversation leaned toward talented musicians, musical performances, and jazz clubs, nationally, each had attended.

Every headliner performed twice in the two-level theater, for one hour each. Once, while the early diners ate, the second time for the early diners.

The passengers were assigned specific show times based upon their dinner seating assignments. Raymond and Loretta were assigned different dinner seating's, but Raymond ignored the assignment and he and Loretta enjoyed the "Early Show", and the late dinner, which was her assigned seating. He was prepared to bribe the gatekeepers but they were lax in inspecting credentials.

The performances were truly outstanding. Monday evening's headliner was saxophonist, Dallas Peoples; a musical legend. Raymond had met Dallas at least thirty years earlier. Elsa Smith, his long-term vocalist, had recently died. Dallas was supported by three of the ship's talented, versatile sidemen; a pianist, drummer and a bassist. It was less expensive to book just the star instead of his group. They had had a thirty-minute rehearsal. Raymond felt his performance was, as usual, excellent: producing "sheets of smooth sound". The sidemen found him easy to support.

Dallas played tenor in the Coleman Hawkins–Lester Young, tradition: smooth and soft; only a generation later, after both of the original "cool" axe men had died earlier. He played mostly old standards in a laid back, jazz motif, which Raymond had heard him perform over the years. After Dallas' performance, Raymond and Loretta went 'backstage' to say hello.

"How you doin' man?" Raymond asked as they smoothed hands. "It's been too long. I guess Trumpet's in New Jersey was the last time I heard you blow; that was back in the 70s?"

"Sssh". Dallas smiled as he placed his forefinger over his lips, "I don't want these young cats to know how old I really am." Raymond was one year older than Dallas, who was eighty-five. They laughed and shared memories for about fifteen minutes.

Say, man." Raymond asked, "When are you going to quit playing gigs? You're already older than dirt!"

"And then what am I going to do, shovel shit into the wind?" Both men laughed heartedly. Dallas continued, "If I was working I would have retired years ago; playing my axe is not work, it's fun; almost as much fun as sex!" Dallas, after apologizing for his "locker room" language, complimented Loretta on her appearance. She graciously accepted while smiling. "We have a sax blow-out scheduled on this cruise," Dallas said to Raymond. "Several of these younger dudes are trying to replace me as the Boss Tenor."

"Hell, you've been 'The Man' for decades, when you replaced Prez and 'The Hawk', but, somebody is going to eventually replace you."

"I know, I know, but not on this cruise!"

"Hell, replacement is inevitable. Prez outplayed 'The Hawk' in his later years, even though Prez passed on before The Hawk, who spent too much time in Europe. Prez was 'The Man' when he died in '59, 'The Hawk', after 'Prez's' death, had Gene 'Jughead' Ammons, Ben Webster, and Sonny Stitt to compete with for top axe honors. The Hawk lost his luster, due to alcoholism and depression in the early fifties; he died in '69, unheralded, as a 'has been.'"

Loretta was impressed with Raymond's knowledge regarding sax legends. He is quoting events that occurred over fifty years ago, as if it was yesterday, to a jazz legend, who has not disputed one fact. Just how deep does his jazz intellect go?

"I've got to make sure my solos are strong and mellow; especially during the 'blow out', which is getting tougher with each gig! You know, I think I'll bypass my solo, so my playing won't be so easily compared with some of these younger dudes."

When I was a passenger on a jazz cruise with Dallas, earlier, we both wound up sitting on the pool deck and started an interesting conversation about business. I was surprised at Dallas' business knowledge, and surprised again, to see him reading the Wall Street Journal between comments. I was also surprised to learn that Dallas had mastered over fifteen different Saxes and clarinets. He probably has several businesses that need his attention. Raymond thought while talking with Dallas.

Raymond and Loretta strolled on the open pool deck; Raymond was enthralled by the brilliance of the stars. Raymond hugged Loretta and attempted to kiss her. Their mouths met but Loretta's lips remained closed.

At eleven, they said goodnight. Musicians played in various lounges until the wee hours with the last session ending at sunrise.

CHAPTER FOUR

THE SECOND MORNING, MONDAY, Raymond and Walter were in the cafeteria at six. Raymond reviewed the cruise's daily activities. There were twenty-six events scheduled from eight a.m. until one a.m; ninety percent were music related. Because of simultaneous scheduling, the seventeen hours of planned activities, plus spontaneous jam sessions, planning one's activities was a herculean challenge, so Raymond was content following Loretta's suggestions. There was a Singles breakfast scheduled at eight-thirty, but Raymond no longer considered himself single so that event was not an option.

At eight-thirty a.m., Raymond called Loretta; there was no answer; he was disappointed. *If she was not in her cabin and was not in the cafeteria, where was she?* Raymond asked himself.

At ten o'clock, the ship made its first island stop, which was Dominican Republic's Samara. There was nothing on board that Raymond and Walter were interested in doing; bingo, whist, and dominoes were not appealing to either of them, especially on a jazz cruise.

Walter wasn't feeling up to par; he had recently had hip surgery and was having trouble walking, so he decided not to go ashore. Raymond, alone, was amongst the first passengers debarking on Samara.

On shore, glancing back, all of the tourist ships looked alike, except for their names, painted on the front of each. It was the first opportunity Raymond had to view the enormity of their vessel; it was at least three blocks long, a half block wide and seventy-five feet tall, not including the antennas, or smokestacks. On board everything was compact, especially the rooms. However, while looking back at the ship from Samara, it was enormous.

There were internationally known retail establishments within a short walk of the pier. Restaurants and bars were everywhere. Attractively dressed, male, and female, hawkers were in front of each establishment.

Raymond walked around aimlessly; the streets were narrow. He stopped in a restaurant and ordered a ham sandwich, but it was not tasty. He ended up eating a cold, seafood lunch and listening to a very talented African American male pianist, who sang while he played; ala Nat King Cole. He was thirtyish, around six feet tall, dressed in summer, washable, attire, with sandals. He was handsome.

"Where you from?" Raymond asked as he slid his chair closer to the musician.

"America." The musician answered, continuing to play.

"Hell, I know that; what city do you call home?"

"As long as we agree I grew up in an American city, what does it matter?"

Raymond realized the pianist was being secretive, maybe for a reason, he surmised.

"I didn't mean to pry, my brother, I was just wondering how a musician as talented as you could end up playing in a nondescript bar in Samara?"

"Life is full of unanswered questions, isn't it?"

"Might I know your name?"

"Another unanswered question," the musician smiled as he continued to play. " Most people call me 'The Piano Man', or '88'."

. "How long have you been playing here?"

"Damn man! Why don't you eat your snack, enjoy the music, and go back to your fucking ship? My life, or how I got here, is none of your business!"

"Okay, man, okay. I meant no harm. Just trying to fill some time off the ship, you know. I'm a writer, and sometimes interesting stories that I hear while travelling wind up in my novels." Raymond looked for his waiter to pay his check and prepared to leave.

"I'm sorry, man. Give me your check; I own this place. There was a cheating wife and her lover found dead after being stabbed several times with a kitchen knife in an American city over ten years ago. I was a promising musician, working regularly, until I came home early from a gig. I signed up as a laborer under an alias, on a freight vessel, and jumped ship here. I established a new identity; money talks on a small island. This business had gone bankrupt when I bought it for cash at a bargain rate.

"I'm sure there is a warrant for my arrest in my previous hometown, but they will never see, or hear from me again. My life is very private. I play the most luxurious resort on this island with my combo on the weekends, and play here alone, as I manage my business, four days a week. I have an assistant manager, who also plays the piano, and fills in for me when I'm away."

"Thanks for the explanation. Your story will probably make my next novel; with some creativity, of course. Your anonymity will remain intact."

The pianist paused, looked long and hard at Raymond, and then said, "You're the first person I have told my story to in ten years; I don't know why I did that; I hope this island and my place of business remains unknown."

"You have my word." Raymond pondered to himself, *how many criminals live secret lives on small islands?*

Within two hours, Raymond returned to the ship. After passing through customs, he returned to the pool deck. There he spied Loretta sitting with Walter, having drinks.

"There you are," Loretta said with delight in her voice.

"What the hell is going on?" Raymond asked. Another couple who had been Loretta's dinner guests the night before were startled by Raymond's stark remark. "Where were you this morning? I called your room around eight thirty and no one answered!"

"I was having breakfast in one of the dining rooms; not that I had to get your permission!"

"I'm sorry. You certainly do not have to get my permission. I was expecting you in the cafeteria and when you didn't show, I was disappointed."

"She called our room, dude, looking for you. I told her you had gone ashore; she suggested we meet here, on the pool deck. Everything's cool," Walter said, telling Raymond in coded conversation to calm down.

Raymond's insecurity embarrassed him. He knew that Walter would never make a pass at Loretta. "Forgive my impoliteness, Loretta. It is obvious that I am falling for you, but you have not given me any reason to believe those feelings are mutual. I missed you this morning, but that is my misfortune, not yours. I apologize."

Loretta looked at Raymond as if he were a misbehaving child, and smiled. She forgave his misplaced possessiveness and considered it flattering. Raymond joined the group. To ease the tension, Walter told a funny story; everyone laughed. For several hours, the five of them enjoyed each other's company.

"Let's you and I take a walk," Raymond said to Loretta.

She agreed without knowing Raymond's destination. They walked to the ship's shops. After arriving, Raymond said, "Pick out something nice."

"You don't have to do this," Loretta said.

"But I want to," Raymond replied. "Often times special people are taken for granted. I appreciate you, and want you to know it."

"I'll look around, but once again, this is not necessary."

"I understand, but please, spoil yourself shopping."

There were male and female clothing boutiques, a perfume salon, and an attractive jewelry shop. CDs of all the performing musicians were available. Loretta was attracted to an expensive necklace.

"Wrap it up," Raymond told the clerk.

"Once again, you don't have to do this." Loretta said.

"I heard you, but I want to. Exceptionalism, which exudes from your pores, is often not rewarded, but should be."

Loretta took off her necklace, put on the new one and smiled deeply.

I did the right thing, Raymond thought. "Did you want a CD of any of the performers?" Raymond asked.

"I'd like one of Rodin."

Raymond bought two, one for each of them.

"You know, these CDs cost the musicians about two dollars each. The ship overprices them for twenty dollars," said Raymond.

"So what else is new? Everything on this ship is overpriced."

After dinner, Raymond and Loretta enjoyed the main theater performance, starring Slim James, one of the stars who played alto. His performance was outstanding; he played notes faster than any musician did since the late Charlie Parker.

The quintet took standards, played the opening choruses, and then each musician took a five-minute solo, backed up by his fellows with subtle riffs, and then returned to the original score. Slim took ten-minute solos.

"I met Slim last cruise," Loretta said. "Then, he was playing with one of the stars; this year he is one. He has a master's from Juilliard. Many critics have called him, the Second Coming, the second Charlie Parker.'"

"I am not surprised; he is very talented. He has a master's degree from Julliard? That is special. Dallas has a bachelor's from New York City College, only because they did not require him to attend classes, back in 'the day' He studied while he was on the road, and turned in his written assignments between gigs. They did not have On Line classes then. I guess a number of younger musicians have college degrees."

"Once dope became 'uncool', most musicians completed their education prior to turning professional. A number of them have studied, and a few have taught music in college," added Loretta.

"I didn't know that."

Loretta felt good about bringing new information to Raymond.

As good as Slim's presentations were, Raymond had trouble staying awake. So immediately following Slim's performance, Raymond headed for his cabin.

The next morning, Wednesday, was a day at sea, heading for St. Thomas, V.I. Raymond and Loretta had a full-service breakfast in one of the dining rooms. Afterwards, they went to the eleventh deck cafeteria where Walter, Camellia, and Howard were enjoying coffee after having eaten a self-service meal.

"There's going to be a quartet performing on the pool deck, outside at noon, that I have been told is exceptional," Loretta said.

"Why don't we go to the pool deck early so we can get good seats?" Raymond suggested; everyone agreed.

It was after ten. The ship's crew was setting up for the noon performance, including electronically. The leader, Ryan Hathaway, was putting his reed on his mouthpiece.

"What are you doing?" Loretta asked.

"I'm putting my axe together. This reed and mouthpiece are major parts of my axe." Loretta extended her hand and Ryan placed his reed in her palm. "Be careful, young lady. Not only is that reed the most important part of my instrument, it is also, like my heart, very fragile."

Loretta ignored the flirtatious comment as she examined the reed. It was two inches by four inches, made of Pinewood.

"It's wet," Loretta said.

"It has to be or else it won't vibrate properly."

"How many different types of reeds are there?" Loretta asked, while carefully turning the reed over in her hand.

"There are five different reed strengths for each of the five main axes," said Ryan as he took the reed from Loretta's hand and very carefully attached it to his tenor's mouthpiece. "It takes years for a professional musician to select the right reed." He then attached the mouthpiece to his horn and began to 'warm up'.

"I've learned a lot; thank you very much," Loretta smiled.

"Put this in your information pouch," Ryan said. "Each musician, based upon his playing technique, and his horn, uses a different reed with his embouchure, to play each axe effectively, and keeps at least two reeds available, should one split.

"With his what?" Loretta asked. The word "embouchure" was foreign to her.

"Listen, this can go on for days, and I've got to blow for at least a half hour before hitting to get my embouchure in shape; embouchures are your lips' structure over your mouthpiece which includes the reed." Ryan said as he started playing scales in various keys. "Oh, one more thing; reeds are technically called aero phone components." Ryan returned to playing scales while being amused at Loretta's befuddled reaction to embouchure, and a reed's technical name.

Ryan moved toward the stage and continued to warm up doing complicated fingerings and riffs.

Loretta thought to herself after listening, *Ryan's performance was outstanding. While not a headliner on this cruise, he pushed himself and was very impressive, he will probably be a headliner next year.* The bright sun and the warm breezes made the music even more enjoyable.

Raymond, Loretta, Walter, Howard, and Camellia enjoyed the hour-long performance. As Ryan left the stage, he gave a friendly wave to Loretta and she waved back.

He is probably one of the axe men Houston is concerned about, thought Raymond.

"I'm going to my cabin to rest and refresh," Loretta said to Raymond, "I'll see you before the early show; we should meet in the cafeteria a half-hour beforehand."

"See you then," Raymond responded. He and Walter grabbed a table opposite the pool, and enjoyed the "eye candy"; after several minutes, both decided they wanted some ice cream.

"So, my brother, where are you heading with Loretta?" Walter asked.

"My intentions are to make that fine woman mine," Raymond answered, "But I don't think she shares my feelings."

"I agree. She is friendly, but only platonically. If you push her romantically you might lose her."

"My feelings for her are so deep that I am content to leave this ship without having been intimate, but I would like a commitment from her that being intimate is probable. Then we can see each other frequently during the coming year, each of us meeting the other's family and close friends, and cementing our relationship on next year's cruise, by getting married."

"Damn! You're really out there, my brother!" a surprised Walter said. "One thing you haven't mentioned; you're more than twenty-five years older than Loretta. Secondly, she is still working, and you have been retired for a decade. In addition, what about your sex lives; you have told me you have not enjoyed traditional sex since your heart operation, , and she probably still enjoys sexual relationships. Another thing, her sister is not here because, from Loretta's perspective, she misbehaved last cruise. Hell, how does a fifty-year-old woman misbehave in the eyes of her sixty-year-old sister? Sounds like a very conservative woman, to me."

"You sure know how to ruin a brother's vacation."

"The other thing you told me is you forced her to kiss you, but she kept her mouth closed! Damn man, she is over sixty and has been married twice. What kind of shit is that?" Walter concluded.

Raymond did not have an answer; her behavior raised many questions; their age variance was a serious obstacle. Walter raises some good points, thought Raymond.

CHAPTER FIVE

"TONIGHT'S PERFORMANCE IS GOING to be a first!" Loretta exclaimed as she and Raymond sat down for dinner in one of the plush dining rooms.

"That really must be something special; what's up," Raymond asked.

"Three electronic keyboard masters are going to play, simultaneously."

Raymond agreed. Each 'conductor' stood behind his electronic keyboard, which resembled a four-legged, four by one foot portable piano, but was much more; it produced the sounds of all of the instruments in an orchestra, by activating various controls.

Each 'conductor' stood behind his keyboard; they began with "Stardust," playing the chorus as if three orchestras were playing the same tune at the same time. While one musician 'soloed', the orchestras played behind him with low, various riffs on different instruments. Their soloist's presentations were spectacular. After thirty minutes, they returned to "Stardust's" chorus, ended the number, paused for applause, and then played Billy Strayhorn's "A Train."

The audience gave them a resounding, standing ovation when they finished, which validated it was a "once in a lifetime" musical spectacle; listening to three virtual orchestras on stage simultaneously: the invisible announcer said, "You just heard the future of Jazz."

After the stellar performance, Walter left; Raymond and Loretta strolled along the deck.

"So Babee, it's a beautiful night with billions of stars in the sky, and fewer satellites; let's take a ride on a rocket."

"What's the difference between a star and a satellite?"

"Simply put, a star reflects the sun's brightness; a satellite revolves around planets. But what I want to know is where are we heading, twinkling, like the stars, or revolving around each other?" Raymond asked as he put his arm around Loretta's waist; they glanced upward into the star-filled sky.

"You sure talk a high level of smack," said Loretta while staring at Raymond, acting disappointed with his banter; but she loved it. "Our next port-of-call is San Juan," Loretta answered while smiling, knowing she was avoiding Raymond's question.

"A high level is relative, as indicated by the stars, satellites, planets, meteors, and comets, miles away, witnessing our relationship develop.

"You mean this is more than a shipboard encounter?" She asked.

"It is to me. I'm looking forward to our spending time together after the cruise."

"Are you planning on moving to Tucson?"

"That's a possibility. I do not have any anchors in Colorado Springs. Would I be welcome?"

"It depends on what 'welcome' means. I would be happy to see you; we could go to church together. I am sure our pastor would welcome a new member. And we have a number of single ladies, closer to your age, who would enjoy meeting someone as handsome, prosperous, and intelligent as you."

"Why do you keep taking yourself out of my equation? If I moved to Tucson, it would be because of my feelings for you."

"That would be impractical. Age does matter. When I retire in five years, at sixty-five, you will be ninety. Besides, I haven't heard you mention anything about your religious commitment which causes me to believe religion is not one of your strong suits: it is one of mine."

"You're thinking too many years ahead; five beautiful years can be the best years of both of our lives; before you retire, or I reach ninety. You seem to be a devout believer in religion, so let us discuss it. I do not believe in a God or a hereafter, or that our world, or, the other universes, were all created in seven days. In the beginning, what made a day? There was no sun or clocks. I realize I am a minority in not believing. But I could accept you as a believer, as long as my commitment of time and money were measured."

"Damn!" Loretta exclaimed, "You are the first Atheist I have met. I am interested in knowing your thinking processes which led you to believe there is no God."

"Sure. Most people, who say they believe in God, and the Hereafter, really do not. People spend fortunes delaying death. If you fear death, then your belief in the hereafter, or God, is limited because you cannot enjoy what you believe in without dying.

"There was a song in the late fifties, whose lyrics proclaimed, 'Everybody wants to go to Heaven, but nobody wants to die'. How true. Catholic priests and nuns celebrate death. Priests at funerals praise 'passing on' as a good thing. Colored Protestants call it 'Coming Home'. Most people treat religion as a social clique.

"Does your religion condone divorces? You have had two. How about dalliances? Most single persons enjoy sex; do you? Most Catholics go to church periodically but not regularly, which is against the Catholic Commandants. Nationally, the average Catholic family is less than three and a half people. That proves Catholics are practicing birth control; again, against Catholic rules. I know some Catholics who have had abortions. It is amazing to me that so many people support a Christian religion, but do what fits regardless of religious constraints. Divorce, Birth control, cheating on expense accounts and taxes, and having occasional dalliances, are just a few of the liberties taken by "believers". They justify their indiscretions with, 'God will understand'. It is amazing that millions of people donate millions of dollars, without a shred of evidence that God, or Heaven, exists.

"I was a devout Catholic when I married, but since then, knowledge regarding man's existence on Earth for twenty million years, the existence of other universes, or galaxies, and my wife's willingness to practice birth control after our two daughters were born, has not allowed me to continue to believe. Once again, I apologize."

"You needn't apologize; I don't feel insulted. You are saying what you have learned and what you believe. Regarding my own beliefs, I don't know what I would do if I didn't attend church regularly."

"Attending church is a good thing, socially. People interact and make lasting friendships; you probably help fellow members through your counsel and contributions. You enjoy singing. Practicing Religion as a lifestyle fills emotional, physical and psychological needs. Without it, many people would have a hole in their emotional structure: a psychological vacuum. However, to believe religion will lead to a life after death is ridiculous!

"What do people in Heaven look like? What does Heaven look like, filled with 20 million years of good people? How many people lived and died during 20 million years? Most religions agree the body stays on Earth when one dies, or it is cremated; that is why cemeteries and mausoleums exist. What does a soul look like? Is the brain part of the soul? Without a brain, you have no memory, or the ability to think or speak. If the brain is not a part of what goes to Heaven, then what does?

;"I know preachers of various Christian faiths that commit adultery, regularly. Catholic priests are notorious for abusing young boys. 'Christians' had no trouble condoning slavery, or committing Adultery with their female slaves, and their wives knew which is also against the Seventh Commandment. That is why there are so many light-skinned Negroes, like me and Walter."

"I have never heard a person talk about religion the way you do. This is really interesting; share more of your thoughts with me."

"Okay; let's look at religion from an astronomical perspective. Astronomers have determined that Earth, which is one of five planets in our Solar System, or Universe, is approximately five hundred, million years old; there are additional solar systems with additional planets further out in space; as far as twenty-six light years away. Scientists have also determined that People have been on Earth for twenty million years."

"How far away is a light year?

"Six trillion miles."

"So what does that mean?" Loretta asked.

"It means that when Bibles were written by the apostles, less than two thousand years ago, the first being completed thirty-five years after Jesus' death, no one had any idea how vast space was. The Bible was first to mentioned Heaven, Hell, and Purgatory. It also means that within the last fifty years, twenty-six light years, or 126 trillion miles into space, has been explored. Other universes have been discovered, but nobody has seen any signs of Heaven, Hell, or Purgatory. Think of how populated all three would be with twenty million years of people! Heaven and those other places came into being through the Catholic Church, approximately only two thousand years ago: that is very recent, astronomically speaking.

"If God created the heavens over five hundred million years ago, and then created only two humans, Adam and Eve, and put them on planet Earth, in a place called the Garden of Eden; then, in a reasonably brief period, He took it all away because Eve bit into an apple? Come on Loretta, really? Why was the apple 'forbidden fruit'? Here is another unsolved mystery: Adam and Eve had two sons, Cain and Able. Cain killed Able, and then married. Where did Cain's wife come from?

"How our world population of almost eight billion, consisting of multiple races, languages, physical variances, and religions evolved has never been explained from a religious perspective; only from Darwinian's theory.

"Here is something else to consider. Anthropologists have determined that Man has been on Earth for millions of years, but just two thousand years ago, God sent Jesus to Earth through Virgin Mary to save the world by having Jesus create a new, religion."

"I'm going to bed!" Loretta said. *He is making me uncomfortable. I am beginning to doubt what I have believed all my life,* she thought.

"One more thought," Raymond said, excited by his anti-preaching. "The Bible stresses, 'love and help thy neighbor', that it is as difficult as an elephant passing through the eye of a needle, for a rich man to enter the Kingdom of Heaven' yet many pastors are rich, and do little to help the poor. How do all of these persons qualify to enter Heaven?

"Another thing: How do so many congregations justify mega churches that cost millions and seat thousands, and support wealthy pastors that have mansions, ultra-expensive wardrobes, and private jets, while ignoring the underprivileged?

"The Catholic Church owns the Vatican City, in Rome. I have seen this place; it has more statues, memorials, and expensive paintings than you can count. Suppose all of the money spent on lavish, religious lifestyles, including expensive real estate and ostentatious churches, was spent helping the poor. When a Catholic Church or school cannot support itself, part of which means contributing to the Vatican, it is closed. Is that how you help the poor?

"All of this worldwide commitment of time, energy, and cash to religion without evidence that there is a God, or a Heaven, seems to be an enormous waste!

"One more thing. In the Catholic Church there is a sacrament called absolution."

"What is *absolution?*"

"It means that you can live a life of sin, which includes committing crimes, rape, torture, and murder; no matter how grave; if you repent before dying, you are guaranteed a place in Heaven. The Godfathers, and all of their underlings, love that."

Loretta knew there were similar forgiveness procedures in her religion. "I have never met a person who has as many profound thoughts about astronomy and religion." Loretta rushed off, very confused.

Well, thought Raymond, *I sure blew this relationship, but I am glad I did. I would rather our relationship end now than months later, after my religious 'shortcomings' become known. I care a great deal for Loretta, but I am not going to mislead her by presenting a false profile. Our major obstacle remains."*

Raymond gazed at the multitude of stars in the sky, while all sorts of thoughts raced through his mind; and then went to bed.

The next morning Raymond woke after a restless night. He replayed his conversation with Loretta and knew he could have blown their relationship. He got up, showered and shaved, then, with little enthusiasm, left his cabin to meet his friends for breakfast.

"Well, this is a surprise," Walter said, as he and Raymond arrived in the cafeteria, finding Loretta, happy to see them.

"I had trouble sleeping. I thought a lot about what you said last night, and realized all you were doing was sharing knowledge that I had asked for, and that you had gathered. The more I reflected on your messages, the more I began to understand, not agree with, but understand your position. You must have spent scores of hours gathering information. I know several of the same types of people. I agree; to most people religion is a comfort zone rather than a lifelong commitment. Maybe I am too committed to my religion. Moreover, I do believe you love me."

Walter, Howard, and Camellia carried on a frivolous conversation involving jazz, ignoring Raymond and Loretta, who were engrossed in each other.

"I don't know what to say," Raymond said. "Last night when you left I thought you were leaving me, but this morning, that doesn't seem to be the case."

"I've got a lot of thinking to do; in the meantime I want to hear more of your thoughts; they obviously come from considerable research."

"I'd like that." Raymond answered.

"I believe you live an honorable life," said Loretta. "I am sure you help those you can afford to help, and you tolerate those who are religious, like me; even I haven't memorized the Ten Commandments! I am sure you live a very wholesome, honorable, life without religion."

"I agree. Now where does that leave us?"

"I'm working on that. I hope I have until the end of the cruise to make that determination."

"Longer, if necessary. As I said last night, I am very interested in spending the rest of my life with you."

Loretta kissed Raymond on the mouth and brushed his lips with her tongue.

Camellia noticed the intimacy of the kiss, discreetly smiled at Howard, indicating a relationship was blossoming.

With Loretta showing up this morning after last nights' revelations, Raymond again had visions of Loretta meeting his relatives and close friends, and him meeting hers. The thought of them getting married next year on this very cruise, became more realistic. They smiled deeply at each other. They were oblivious to the three additional persons at their table. Walter and Howard were enjoying recalling jazz musicians and musical occasions of years gone by. Camellia was watching the relationship between Raymond and Loretta bloom. All enjoyed breakfast.

"There is a special performance this afternoon, in the 'theatre'," Loretta said.

"Say no more, we're in." Raymond said.

"It is a 'saxophone showdown'," Loretta explained. "There will be eight saxophonists on stage, six tenors, one alto, and one baritone, with a 'boss' rhythm section."

At two, the emcee introduced the performers. Their bios indicated some had played with famous bandleaders, and a few had headed their own groups. Two of the Tenor players were women. Each performer stood and slightly bowed; treating his/her axe as an essential part of their body. Each then returned to their high, bar seat.

At eighty-four, Dallas Peoples was the oldest amongst them while "Slim Daniels", Loretta's new friend, was the youngest. She assumed he had never played with such an array of accomplished axe-men and should have been looking forward to the event.

The ship's music director put Dallas in charge. He decided on the numbers they would play, solo lengths, which were no more than five minutes, and their order of performance.

The base player, as expected, set and maintained the tempo; their first number was Charlie Parker's "Dues in Blues", an up-tempo jazz standard. The rhythm section increased its riffs when the soloist laid back; they played a compatible eight bars. Each saxophonist played the chorus at the same tempo, but created a slightly different sound.

At down times, musicians would challenge each other by playing records and asking fellow musicians to name soloists on various instruments without reading the labels. The musicians' variances were as different as people's voices.

Seldom do musicians play with their peers. Each one was pushing himself to be impressive to fellow sax players they admired, as well as the audience. Listeners pointed forefingers and said, "Where did that come from?" A series of, "Aw mans," emanated over smiles between musicians, during their performance. The two women held their own, they justified being there. Each soloist stood and moved forward before playing. When he/she finished, he/she bowed slightly and returned to their seat, receiving plaudits and gestures that they had played well. The solos were unbelievable.

Their second number was a blues classic "After Hours". Slow, blues riffs prevailed. Dallas' solo was exemplary. The jazz audience enjoyed the blues number, by waving their hands and humming, even though "After Hours" was not jazz. All of the sax players played low, whole note, key compatible, refrains for eight bars, followed by sixteen bars of silence, when the soloists put forth their best musical efforts.

As "After Hours" ended, Dallas suggested the musicians play "Salt Peanuts," with a twist. All the participants played individual solos together. Twenty bars later, they stopped playing and sang, "Salt Peanuts, Salt Peanuts," then returned to their solos. It was a cacophony of sound and rhythms; the audience laughed, enjoyed, and listened to ten minutes of musical mayhem. Slim Daniels lost his concentration, but was delighted with the experience. After ending the number, the group received a standing ovation.

Raymond and his friends left the theatre with musical riffs and solos ringing in their ears. "Did you notice that Dallas only played supportive riffs during 'After Hours' and the 'Salt Peanuts' number?" Raymond questioned his group.

"I wondered why he didn't take earlier soloes," Howard asked.

"He didn't want to be compared to the other players," Raymond answered.

"Why not?" asked Howard.

"This is just conjecture, but Dallas has been the number one 'cool sax man' since Prez died, forty years ago; him being compared with younger sax men just might put his reputation as 'The Tenor Man' in jeopardy," Raymond said. He did not mention the conversation he and Dallas had earlier.

CHAPTER SIX

RAYMOND AND LORETTA WALKED along the decks watching their ship part the water. They stepped into a lounge to have a drink and talk while two musicians were "rehearsing".

Dallas Peoples and the pianist that Raymond had heard playing by himself his first night aboard, Luther Long, were challenging each other, playing difficult riffs while talking and laughing. They were old friends who enjoyed spending time together. They were on the stage of an almost empty lounge.

Gradually, passengers entered the lounge, attracted by the spontaneous, unconnected, riffs. It was a rare privilege for jazz buffs to hear professional musicians practice.

"Say, man," Raymond, who with Loretta, had taken seats near the stage, said to Dallas, "You two are attracting an audience."

"But we're not playing anything," Dallas answered.

"Well, why don't you play something and give your limited audience a musical treat to remember?"

Dallas looked at Luther; they silently agreed that an unexpected performance by two of the most competent men in the 'business' would be in order. "What do you want to hear?" Dallas asked Raymond.

"Where is your support group?" asked Raymond.

"On vacation. It is less expensive for the ship's musical director to hire only Luther, and me than to include our combos. The ship's sidemen are very competent."

"How about playing 'Lush Life'?"

"Man, that's a tough one. You know, Billy Strayhorn wrote that one for himself," Dallas said.

"Here's the real deal," Luther said. "I heard from Billy himself that Duke Ellington, and him, while travelling in their private rail car, in the wee hours, were having drinks and piano doodling, when Billy commented, "We sure are living the lush life, Duke."

Luther continued. "It was during the thirties, with Jim Crow laws prevalent throughout the South; when Negroes were segregated, persecuted, and hung, but Billy, Duke, and his orchestra, were travelling First Class in their two private rail cars; one for sleeping, and relaxing, the other for rehearsing. Duke agreed with Billy's interpretation of their lifestyle, and commented, "This is how the President travels," as Duke ordered another cocktail. The phrase, "Lush Life", stuck with Billy. Before daybreak, Billy had composed a sophisticated number he named 'Lush Life'. Duke liked the number and added his touch.

"Months later, while Billy was playing his new tune, backstage, at a Manhattan gig before show time, Zara Larrson, an attractive, Caucasian, female singer, heard it, liked it, asked when and under what circumstances it was written; then she wrote the unusual lyrics, based upon Billy's input and her having been alone too long.

Luther concluded, ""Lush Life" was introduced by Billy Strayhorn and sung by Kay Davis, with Duke Ellington's Orchestra, at Carnegie Hall in 1948. Since then scores of top musicians and singers have recorded it".

"That's a hell of a story, man, even if it's not true," teased Raymond.

Luther leered contemptuously at Raymond as he then started playing "Lush Life's" chords with Dallas adding short riffs. Luther got "into it," he played for ten minutes; Dallas added chords occasionally. After Luther's extended performance, he nodded toward Dallas who started playing "Lush Life's" theme at the end of Luther's last chorus; who switched to short chord-compatible riffs. They played for about a half-hour, between choruses, switching the lead between them, and ended jointly playing "Lush Life's" main theme. It was a unique musical experience for the limited audience who gave them a standing ovation when they finished.

"How many times does one hear a pianist and a tenor man "knock out" a popular but difficult jazz tune?" Said Raymond. Luther and Dallas complimented each other. They were pleased with their spontaneous, unrehearsed, performance.

"You should have recorded that that was something special!" Shouted a listener.

"If we had, we'd have to pay Duke's and Billy's estates' royalties," Dallas yelled back over a smile. Luther added, "We'll still have to send them something for playing it on this cruise, even before this limited audience. That's how composers get paid."

Raymond and Loretta resumed their casual walk around the ship. "So what kind of thoughts are you having, Babee?" Raymond said, looking into Loretta's eyes.

"It's hard for me to have serious thoughts under such relaxing circumstances," Loretta said.

"I agree. It is difficult to think rationally while on a cruise. A cruise eliminates reality; makes everything possible; a cruise is a fantasy."

"Are you saying your interest in me is a fantasy?"

"Oh, no! Well, I am not sure. We are under the influence of 'the good life'. The crew is treating us royally. The meals are fantastic. This is indeed an unrealistic experience; even our ages seem to be irrelevant."

"So maybe life-changing decisions shouldn't be made under these circumstances," Loretta said.

"Maybe you're right. Perhaps we should wait until our emotions are back to normal," Raymond said, "but that doesn't mean we have to restrict our activities while at sea; maybe we can interact in a way that may assist us in making lasting decisions later on."

"Wow! That was the smoothest sex request I have heard to date," Loretta laughed.

"I was trying to be delicate, and at the same time, persuasive."

"Even though I am sixty and have been married twice, sex to me is still a meaningful event. My participating, if I participate, will be important rather than, like my sister, spontaneous and frivolous." *Perhaps my standards have been too high,* thought Loretta.

"I see," Raymond said, realizing Loretta had considerably reduced the possibility of sex on this cruise. *Sex to her,* Raymond realized, *is not incidental, or non-consequential.*

"Shall we have dinner together?" Loretta asked. She realized she had deflated Raymond's sexual objectives, but did not know whether she had defused his attraction for her.

"Of course," Raymond said, "We still have a lot of living to do. I am going to take a nap so I can hang through the major performance after dinner. See you later." *I have not enjoyed traditional sex in over a decade. I can wait; especially since it is such a major event for Loretta.*

Loretta and Raymond met before dinner in the cafeteria. They decided to eat in the ships elaborate, expensively furnished, dimly lit, Japanese restaurant. Raymond was surprised that a Hamburger in Japanese was called a Kobe; so was a belated basketball star; Kobe Bryant.

After dinner, the evening's primary entertainment was a quartet led by an alto saxophonist; with three of the ship's sidemen; a Congo player, a guitarist, and a pianist, sitting in. They were spectacular and played for about an hour.

After the performance, Raymond and Loretta strolled to the fantail deck, found themselves embracing on the rail and passionately kissing. "I had better go to my cabin before I lose my self-control," Loretta said.

"If losing your self-control means having sex and that is not what you want to do, then I agree," Raymond said, pausing between passionate kisses.

Raymond went to his and Walter's cabin, mentally arguing with himself, wondering if he had done, and said, the right thing.

"I didn't think I was going to see you tonight, man" Walter smiled. "I thought Loretta might have invited you to her cabin."

"There you go, thinking again. Some things are more important than sex, like lasting relationships," Raymond said.

"Sex and lasting relationships are very compatible under normal circumstances, of course Loretta is an exceptional woman," Walter responded.

"Good night my brother! And you're right; Loretta is not normal, she is much more than that!" Raymond said as he turned his back toward Walter's single bed.

The next morning Loretta participated in the exercise program on the fantail deck with seven other women and one male. She then had breakfast in one of the dining rooms with her friends. Raymond and Walter ate in the cafeteria. Howard and Camellia were sleeping in; they had listened to a jam session that started around midnight and lasted until three a.m. Their next port of call was St. Thomas; the largest island on the schedule.

Raymond was once again disturbed when he could not find Loretta, but he behaved. After breakfast, he strolled along the deck and ran into Loretta and her friends. "Are you going ashore today?" Raymond asked casually.

"Yes. We are going into St. Thomas in about an hour; would you like to come along?"

"No. I think I'll stay on board and participate in the bid whist tournament." Raymond did not want to share Loretta with her friends.

Loretta realized playing Bid Whist was not what he really wanted to do. "Why don't you two go on without me? I'll stay with Raymond." Loretta's friends departed.

"Why are you changing your plans?" Raymond asked.

"I heard the disappointment in your voice. I thought I should stay with you so we could talk." They found a table for two, outside, under an umbrella, which sheltered them from the tropical sun.

"I purposely avoided you this morning because I felt unsure of my self-control last night. I had decided that I wasn't going to submit to you onboard; but last night, after our embraces, enlightening conversation, and passionate kissing, I wasn't sure."

"I don't know how to respond, nor do I know how you want me to respond. Our having sex does not include your being submissive. If that is what you want to do, we would be sharing a pleasant event. There is nothing I want more than to have sex with you, but not if you are going to feel guilty about it. What you are saying is you also want to have sex but your religious commitment says you should not; am I right?"

"I think so." *This dude is different, exciting and enticing.*

"Well, let me put your mind at rest. I will not attempt to seduce you, onboard. These circumstances are not normal and I am willing to wait until the cruise is over. Tucson is only a half-hour from Colorado Springs, by jet."

"Oh, Raymond, I really appreciate your saying that. My fondness for you is increasing."

"However, if you insist, I would be less than a gentleman if I didn't comply," Raymond said while laughing aloud.

Loretta laughed, "You don't know how close you are to getting laid."

"You're right. And there is only one way for me to learn the reality of my circumstance."

"Okay, okay. That is enough of that! Let's talk about something else."

Raymond reached across their small table and took both of Loretta's hands, "I am falling in love with you, Loretta; while sex is essential, making love with you is far more significant."

Loretta held Raymond's hands, and smiled brilliantly through bright eyes. *His distinguishing between having sex and making love was very impressive.*

"Let's go join the bid whist tournament," Raymond said. Loretta agreed.

The game lasted for two hours; Loretta and Raymond won third place out of fifty pairs of players.

The after-dinner performance was, once again, spectacular. The star's name was Vera Long, who sang as she played the piano. Four of the ship's sidemen supported her. Vocally, she was a cross between Billie Holliday and Sarah Vaughn: Billie's unique phrasing, and Sarah's clear voice and immense range, which was an unusual four octaves. Vera's piano technique reminded Raymond of Errol Gardner; who never took a piano lesson; competent, but not overwhelming. She played and sang most of Billie and Sarah's classics. Her ship's musicians laid back appropriately. They remained silent when she sang sensitive parts of torch songs, played soft, supportive riffs when she sang choruses, or laid into her piano skills.

It seemed her hour-long performance was not long enough; the audience insisted she play and sing an encore. "I can't wait to hear her perform again; if she's fortunate enough to find a songwriter who can write songs to fit her range and style, she may become an 'overnight' sensation ... or maybe she could write them herself," said Raymond, remembering that Peggy Lee had written over two hundred songs. "Check the agenda and see if she is performing on board again."

"That was her second gig. She had a midnight show Tuesday, where she performed by herself," Loretta said after checking the itinerary.

"Damn!" exclaimed Raymond. They walked arm-in-arm to Loretta's cabin. He waited for Loretta to open her door; she did not. Raymond and Loretta said a romantic goodnight; hugging and kissing more passionately than the night before, flush against her locked, cabin door.

Raymond did not ask Loretta to open her door. He felt their passionate embraces and wet, tongue-filled kisses were leading to something more. If he had asked she may have complied, but he did not want her to feel guilty, or to overly influence her.

They said goodnight over continued, long, smoldering kisses. *I should have invited him in,* thought Loretta, immediately after Raymond had left.

CHAPTER SEVEN

IT WAS THURSDAY, DAY six of the cruise. Walter and Raymond, because of stormy weather, stumbled while walking through the narrow halls, bouncing off walls as they headed for the elevators. The First Mate had announced, their ship was entering the outer boundaries of a powerful hurricane.

After reaching the cafeteria, they gasped as they saw the blowing rain and rough seas through the massive windows. Anchored tables were stationary but everyone was having trouble balancing their china.

"It's amazing," said Walter to Raymond, "That a ship this massive can be tossed about like a rowboat by an angry sea."

"Sure, you're right."

Walter and Raymond stepped cautiously through the food lines, poured themselves half cups of coffee, half glasses of juice, and staggered toward their tables.

Eating and drinking was a challenge. It was six, and as daylight increased, the views of the storm grew even more alarming.

"Attention please," a voice said over the public speaker. "We are sailing threw a hurricane; it will worsen throughout the day. We recommend that everyone stay inside. Venturing outside will get you very wet and possibly swept overboard. There will be an unscheduled movie shown at ten. We are bringing the afternoon music presentation inside, and are rescheduling the evening performance. Please know that no matter how torrential the weather, this vessel is secure. Thank you."

"Well," said Raymond, "it looks like we are in for a very rough day. I think they are showing the movie to take our minds off the storm."

"I agree," Walter answered. "Since we are alone, let's discuss Loretta; where are you two heading?"

"That's a good question. Just when I think we are developing a relationship, something happens and the progress dwindles."

"How strong are your feelings for her?"

"Pretty strong. At times, I feel as though I want to marry her, then at other times, because of her reaction to something, I have said or done, marriage seems unrealistic. She has societal airs, you know."

"Yeah, it's called education," said Walter. Although both were very astute businesspersons, neither had completed college.

"You have been alone for almost two years, and I think Loretta is the first woman you have emotionally encountered since Jean died. Are you sure you are falling in love or are you just filling a void?

"I don't know; what do you think?"

"Loretta is a nice person, and she looks good for a sixty-year-old; but from my perspective I'm not sure you two are in love, or, even compatible. She seems to be more comfortable with me than she is with you."

"I agree; I have noticed her response to you during our conversations, and your frequently shared laughs; she places a high value on laughing, you know. I think it is because she knows you are married, and morally righteous, so there is no risk of you hitting on her, and she is aware of my intentions, which are substantive. Besides, you are the better raconteur. I am more serious and direct, less talkative. Moreover, she certainly has not agreed that we should become one. I think I am going to have to wait until this cruise is over before I can get a commitment from her."

"Are you sure that's what you want?"

"No, I'm not sure; that's why I am willing to wait! I think she is what I want, but a cruise is the wrong place to make lifelong decisions. Serious thinking should not exist aboard ship. Waiting at least a month or so after this cruise is over is probably the best thing. Her not wanting to jump into bed with me might be wise."

"Another consideration is your age variance. Before she retires at sixty-five, you will be ninety. That is, if you're still around."

"Yeah, I've thought about that, too. Hell, I do not even know if I can perform if she does give it up. You know I have not had a normal, sexual relationship in over twenty years, since my heart surgery. I do enjoy her company though, but I'm not sure what our romantic interludes would resemble; whether they would reflect love, age, or the absence of loneliness."

"And then there's that church thing," continued Walter. "Jean put up with you not going to church, but you don't know what Loretta's attitude will be."

"I became a devout Catholic before our marriage. Three years in, an event occurred. Jean and I never discussed it, and I haven't discussed it with anyone over the sixty years we were married."

"I'm listening."

"I don't know if I'm ready to discuss it now."

"If you're not going to talk about it with me, then with whom, and when?"

"Okay, I'll make it quick. After our second child was born, Jean insisted that we practice Birth Control, which was against Catholic doctrine. If that was to become our lifestyle, then we were violating our religious commitment; which meant to me, I could ignore any and all segments of our religious commitment," answered Raymond.

"Well, good morning," Walter said to Howard and Camille. It was eight o'clock.

"I think I'll call Loretta," Raymond said.

Upon returning to their table, Raymond said, "She's feeling seasick, and has decided to stay in her cabin."

The four of them silently watched the rain, sea, and wind intensify. They listened to the muffled roar of the bottomless sea, while "elevator" music played. Howard took photos of his awe-struck peers, and the storm beating on the immense, cafeteria windows.

"Good morning," First Mate Solomon Van Batten said, as he stood before their table; "It is so refreshing to see African Americans on board. Are you comfortable?.

"I noticed your accent, where are you from?" asked Camellia.

"I'm from Scotland," the First Mate answered. "I thought I had lost my accent," he smiled.

"Why yes, we are comfortable; shouldn't we be? Moreover, why is our being Black refreshing? Raymond asked.

"The larger cruise liners schedule at least ten themed cruises, annually: bridge, ballroom dancing, Rock 'n' roll, classical music, showing professional sports-oriented games with celebrities, some of whom played in the events, narrating them, and more. But regardless of the featured events, most ships have less than one percent African American passengers," the First Mate answered.

"The only time there are significant numbers of African American passengers is on jazz cruises. We appreciate your presence because you are a happier lot, making the cruise more enjoyable for the crew as well as yourselves. And yes, you certainly should be comfortable, but people who aren't familiar with cruises might develop a needless fear because of the foul weather we are experiencing."

"Ray and Walt might be comfortable, but I'm scared to death! As much as we cruise, this is our first hurricane; are we sailing into one?" Camellia nervously inquired.

"We are in a large hurricane now; it's too wide to circumvent, but don't be concerned. There are 320 ocean-going cruise ships worldwide, carrying over eleven million passengers annually. No cruise ship has ever been negatively impacted by a storm, no matter the ferocity."

"So all of the lifeboats and the drills we had before sailing are just for show, huh?" Camellia asked.

"'Sailing' is an acceptable misnomer; sails on ships no longer exist, but the term is still used. Multiple, powerful, gas-powered engines power ships. The drills are performed to comply with

International Maritime regulations that have not been revived in generations."

"So the worst that will happen is that some of us will get sea-sick?" asked Howard.

"Probably, but being aboard ship, like life itself, has certain risks. Sixteen people died onboard cruise ships between 2005 and 2011; that is one death per twelve million passengers. All were due to natural causes. In 2017, there were five overboard incidents; suicide might have been the cause for several, although none were proven; how do you prove a suicide? For passenger security, every vessel has at least one jail cell and a minimum of two experienced firearms personnel because, as it is with every large gathering, people might misbehave. Of course, the chance of being seriously hurt, or killed, on a cruise ship exceeds eleven million to one. Jazz cruises, have even fewer negative experiences."

"I have read about serious plagues aboard ship," Walter said.

"Yes, there have been several, and they are very detrimental to the cruise industry."

Solomon Van Batten stood, straightened his uniform and said, "You folks enjoy your cruise; it was pleasant talking with you."

"Right on, hurricane or not, full speed ahead!" Camellia said to Solomon, stabbing her fist into the air, while smiling. Solomon smiled back, and returned her fist gesture. The foursome resumed observing the storm; they felt much more secure. Solomon introduced himself to another group of passengers.

The morning turned into afternoon. The foursome had sandwiches and salads for lunch. "Let's take a walk," Raymond said to Walter. They went to the third level, where most of the musicians shared cabins. One lounge's door read; "Musicians Only".

Raymond said to Walter, "Let's go see what Dallas is doing; we look like musicians, don't we?"

"Old ones at best," Walter answered.

They walked in; no one paid them any attention. Musicians were still wearing sleeping gear. They were having coffee, juice, croissants and bowls of fruit. Some were humming as they reviewed sheets of music. The headliners had suites, shared by wives or companions. They joined their "kin" in the lounge for Musicians Only, to enjoy the commonality.

"You know," Raymond said, noticing Walter's surprise at the musicians still wearing nightclothes, "Our evening is their afternoon and they don't get sleepy, especially if they are jamming, until around four in the morning."

Dallas's friend, Luther, was playing "Stormy Weather" on the anchored piano, adding chords when appropriate. A drummer took the seat behind the anchored drums, and accompanied Luther's playing with brushes. A bass player carried his instrument onto the stage and "came in" appropriately. He started sliding across the stage, after seating himself, holding on to his bass while playing, laughing continuously. A guitar player and an alto saxophonist stepped onto the stage. Everyone was laughing between riffs. Some musicians quit eating, went to their cabins and returned playing "Stormy Weather" chords.

Their playing while "shifting" was a new experience. Two additional saxophonists joined the group. Raymond and Walter took seats to enjoy the "moving" jam session..

Dallas entered the lounge, saw Raymond and Walter, and joined them. He was wearing a casual ensemble, with sandals; he had heard the music when he stepped out of his suite, two levels above. He was not carrying his "axe". "They're having fun," he said.

"Why don't you join them, man?" asked Raymond.

"That's not in my contract. I quit 'sitting-in' twenty years ago," Dallas said.

Raymond had never seen Dallas play in a jam session. "What's wrong with 'jamming', man?" asked Raymond.

Dallas took a sip of coffee and then said, "There are two thousand passengers on this ship that spent approximately four thousand dollars each to be here; and they'll probably spend another $500 on gifts, drinks and souvenirs. Hell! That is almost ten million dollars, man! The ship's executives negotiated hard with my agent for me to play three sets while on board. If they want me to participate in a jam session, then pay me. This is not a sentimental journey, man, this is business; and I don't play for free!"

"What were you and Luther doing when you played 'Lush Life' the other day, man"?

"We started out rehearsing. Hell that was fun! Besides, you asked us to play that."

Dallas thinks more like a business executive than most musicians do, Raymond decided. He probably emulates Ray Charles when it comes to managing his money. Ray Charles died with a net worth of over seventy-five million dollars. He was probably one of the most financially successful Black musicians, ever.

"Attention, attention on board, please," the public address system announced, "because of the inclement weather, we are changing today's musical format." There will be an unscheduled Jam Session at noon in the Wayward Lounge."

"I knew if I looked long enough, I'd find you two," Loretta said as she entered the musicians' Day Room.

Wow! Thought Raymond. It took a herculean effort to find us here. Just when I think our relationship is fading, she does something like this. "They just announced a new program for this afternoon's entertainment. Let's go get seats for the set."

Loretta agreed. As Raymond rose from his seat, Loretta grabbed his hand and smiled. Raymond was pleased with her expressed affection, but was very confused.

When they arrived at the Wayward Lounge, the stagehands were anchoring the piano and drums into floor brackets. Two chairs for a guitarist and a bassist were also anchored. Brass and reed instrumentalists were required to balance themselves as they played. The impromptu session jammed, during which twenty musicians participated. Slim James, on alto and clarinet, was outstanding. The additional players were demonstrative in their appreciation. Slim James was getting closer to sounding like "The Man". Someone shouted, "Charlie Parker lives!"

The evening performance was also changed. There were eight pianists on board; paired off by the musical director, who decided on the piano duos and their musical agenda. Each pair would play a classical jazz number, like "Lush Life", or "Mood Indigo", and then an up tempo piece, like "One O'clock Jump", or, Cherokee. The audience enjoyed the sidemen's brief solos, as well as the fifteen-minute solos of each pianist.

The audience heard note combinations, AKA, riffs, made famous by Errol Garner, George Shearing, Duke Ellington, Art Tatum, Dorothy Donnegan, and Count Basie, while the pianists played their fingers off.

"This is the only time and place you can hear this much piano" said Raymond to Loretta. Each pair stretched their playing ability, knowing that there was not only a critical audience, but also peer pianists in the "wings," and a fellow pianist, also playing his heart out, just ten feet away, which was quite unusual. It was a unique musical occurrence.

The audience left happily discussing whom they had enjoyed the most, never having heard eight of the nation's best pianists play in one set.

Loretta and Raymond, after the "piano jam", kissed passionately outside her cabin door. Raymond, after a long, deep kiss, walked away. Loretta was left wanting.

CHAPTER EIGHT

RAYMOND AND WALTER HAD been up since six, having coffee and … enjoying an outstanding daybreak; with the sun "coming out" of the ocean. As soon as daylight emerged, they went on the pool deck, and commandeered a table to enjoy the sun's rising, and the tropical breezes. Howard and Camellia joined them around seven-thirty. They had been up until three a.m., enjoying a jam session.

Friday was a beautiful summer day. The water's surface was smooth as glass, save for the ship's wake. There was not a cloud in the sky. More musicians were on the pool deck, absorbing the sunshine and inhaling the salt air while blowing "nothings" on their horns, after having been sequestered the day before. Several musicians were playing standard jazz tunes and introducing unusual riffs instead of practicing difficult fingerings. Because they were partially secluded, the music sounded like the ocean was jamming.

"Where's Loretta?" Camellia asked Raymond.

"Beats me," answered Raymond, smiling. He was flattered by Camellia's insinuation that he should know Loretta's whereabouts.

"Good morning, everybody!" Loretta said as she joined the group. She ran her hand over Raymond's chest and then around the back of his neck, from behind his chair. She then bent over and kissed him on the lips with her mouth open. Camellia smiled; her eyes widened. She looked at Howard to see if he had noticed; he had not.

"What are you having for breakfast, dear? Is it appropriate for me to call you dear?" asked Raymond.

"Well now," answered Loretta, "That depends on your intentions." Camellia laughed aloud.

"My intentions have been clear since the first day of our voyage. You are the mysterious one."

"I'm aware of your desires and objectives, but not your intentions."

"Oh my goodness; where's my Thesaurus? After you eat we will move to someplace private and I will expound upon my intentions, desires, and objectives until you clearly understand," Raymond said.

"Can I be a fly on the wall?" asked Camellia, and everyone laughed heartedly.

"Why don't we go to one of the dining rooms where I'll have breakfast and you can elaborate on your intentions?" Loretta asked.

"See you folks after we agree, at least grammatically," said Raymond.

"Be sure to take notes," Camellia smiled.

Howard lightly punched Camellia in the ribs, and said, "The reason they are leaving is to keep their conversation private."

"Now why didn't I realize that?" Camellia answered. She was having fun; to Camellia, nothing was more exciting than a developing romance.

After Loretta ordered breakfast, and Raymond ordered a croissant with coffee, she said, "Besides bedding me, what else do you have in mind?"

That is a complicated question, thought Raymond. She knows I have wanted to make love to her since we said hello. Our romantic kisses last evening must have stirred her hormones. Obviously, she wants a commitment past the cruise; we dock tomorrow; tonight is our last night! How badly do I want to be intimate with her? Will I be able to perform satisfactorily? She seems amenable.

I have not had a normal sexual relationship in over twenty years Raymond continued to ponder. *If I suggest going to bed, I think she will agree, but what will be the result? If I do not suggest going to bed, how will Loretta react? I think I will let her make the decision.*

"Babee, my feelings for you have increased with each day, including being intimate. However, if our 'getting into it' will have a major influence on our life together, I would like to wait until the circumstances are more desirable. One night on a cruise can be misleading. If, however, our being intimate is something you are looking forward to, and it would not be a major decision-making event, then I would want to make love to you tonight."

"So it's *my* decision, huh?"

"It has always been your decision. I just do not want it to be too important. I would rather it be an extension of our being romantic, rather than it determining our future."

"So, our having sex should be a natural flow rather than establishing a base for our continued relationship?" asked Loretta.

"Let's just say our making love would be an extension of our sharing passionate kisses; those are my thoughts, what's yours?"

"What you are saying is our initial sexual relationship would be an extension of our social experiences, like dancing?"

"Yes. Leaving it to be improved upon, like learning how to dance together, better, after our first dance, rather than deciding our first dance is the best we can do."

"We both might be surprised," Loretta said, while smiling wickedly.

"We might be."

"Okay," Loretta said, "let's 'sleep' together tonight, and see how we feel tomorrow morning, before we part."

Yeahhh, thought Raymond. He added, *I think.*

It was early afternoon. A quartet was playing in one of the smaller lounges; Raymond and Loretta decided to listen.

The saxophonist had an alto sax, a tenor, a baritone, and a flute. The pianist had hooked up a second keyboard, which was a portable organ. The guitarist also had a bass guitar and a viola. The drummer had extensive drum sizes, a string of musical, metal tubes, a very large symbol, plus three, four-foot conga drums, and a small lap set. The group could present any musical style.

Each number sounded completely different. After their third selection, the leader said, "Ladies and gentlemen, we have a gifted song stylist amongst us; not a professional, but gifted nonetheless. With your encouragement maybe she will favor us with a song."

The audience applauded enthusiastically; with Raymond's encouragement, Loretta walked to the stage.

After telling the leader her key, she set the tempo with the bassist, and then sang, "My Funny Valentine." She sang it beautifully in a slow tempo, with no strained notes, with just enough jazz phrasing to make it a tonal, romantic presentation; she sang in perfect pitch, like Ella Fitzgerald, using an unusually wide vocal range, like Sarah Vaughn.

She sang two verses, after which the band members played solos each for five minutes while Loretta slightly danced, and encouraged the audience to applaud after each solo. It was clear Loretta was an experienced jazz singer, especially with a small group. Loretta, after repeating the verses, closed out the number to a standing ovation. The audience pleaded, but Loretta refused to sing a second number. After returning to her seat, Loretta said, "That was dedicated to you, baby."

"You sounded great!" Said Raymond, "Why didn't you do more than one song?"

"Musical union regulations dictate no musician 'sitting in' may sing or play more than two numbers. I like to leave my audiences wanting more; one was enough. I sing in my church's choir, at weddings and funerals. I only sing jazz songs at festivals or on cruises."

"*She is an experienced jazz singer,* concluded Raymond. He said, "You could sing professionally. Surely your congregates appreciate your availability."

"They do. I never mention compensation. Some of my more affluent church members have gifted me, which I graciously accept, but it's not a requirement."

This woman's mine, thought Raymond, *I have no idea how versatile and talented she really is,* he thought as they enjoyed the rest of the quartet's performance.

Raymond and Loretta stopped to listen to a different group playing in a different lounge, but after five minutes, decided they were not worth their time because they were more Rock 'n' rollers, and tasteless comedians, rather than aspiring jazz musicians. Raymond silently wondered how, and why, they were booked on a jazz cruise.

The couple enjoyed snacks as a late lunch. They continued to stroll about the ship having pleasant, non-committal, conversations. They ended up on the Pool Deck with Walter, Howard, and Camellia.

"You don't need to tell me what was said," Camellia said. "I can tell by your body language; it was very pleasing to both of you."

Loretta and Raymond glanced at each other, slightly embarrassed.

"See! I told you, I told you! What a beautiful way to end a cruise!"

Camellia was as excited as if SHE had just fallen in love.

"Why don't you let people tell you what they want you to know, instead of telling people what you believe you know?" asked Howard.

"It's obvious they are in love. If you cannot see that, you are blind!" Camellia was upset with Howard.

"Forgive my wife, folks, she is such a romantic, she fantasizes even when she has no idea what she is talking about."

"Congratulations," Camellia said to Raymond and Loretta, then she threw a snide look towards her husband, which said, "I told you so."

Walter remained silent, closely observing his best friend, as well as Loretta.

"Let's go find some music to listen to; this is a jazz cruise, right?" said Raymond, almost blushing.

Loretta smiled at Camellia, silently saying, "What else can I do?" as she rose from her seat while Raymond pulled her up by her hand. Camellia understood.

"How musically hungry are you?" Raymond asked.

"Not very. Besides my yearnings are not about music or eating."

"Suppose we visit your cabin, and skip dinner?"

"Well, it's about time you asserted yourself."

75

CHAPTER NINE

BE CAREFUL WHAT YOU wish for, Raymond thought as he and Loretta held hands outside her cabin, not speaking, glancing at each other, both anxiously contemplating what was about to happen. *I have not experienced traditional sex in twenty years. Moreover, I have no idea how I am going to perform, or how she is going to respond.*

"Well, what do you want to do?" Loretta said, smiling. She opened the door with her key card, and turned on the light. There was one double bed. Raymond pulled his T-shirt off, and started unfastening his belt buckle. Loretta turned off the light. Because there was no porthole, the room went black. *I do not want my body to be on display*, she thought. They both continued undressing blindly.

Their hands explored each other's anatomy while standing, feeling each other's protrusions. Raymond's penis brushed her vagina as he held her close. He grabbed her butt cheeks and kissed her passionately.

Loretta disengaged, turned, and pulled back the blanket and sheet. She then laid her body down. With outstretched arms, while smiling, she beckoned to Raymond; her body, smile, and outstretched arms became slightly visible; he complied. Their tongues battled more intensely than before; she won. He explored her body with his hands, caressing her ample breasts, stroking her vagina while continuing to kiss. Raymond pulled her close. Loretta fondled his soft penis.

Raymond moved his lips to her breasts. Loretta sighed, still massaging his penis; it grew larger. Raymond lowered himself against her body, distancing her hand from his penis as he kissed and tongue-bathed her anatomy, including her butt; moments later, his tongue reached her vagina; Loretta gasped.

"Oh, baby," Loretta moaned, "that feels wonderful." Her hands were massaging his head, occasionally sticking her fingers in his ears. Raymond became more aggressive, tonguing and devouring her vagina and rectum, stimulating her even more. Moments later, continuing his tonguing activity, he began shifting his body until they were in the sixty-nine position.

"What are you doing?" Loretta asked. Her question did not require an answer; his moves were clear. She shifted her body under his.

"Maybe I'm asking too much. If you're uncomfortable, I'll understand."

"Obviously you want me to give you head?"

"Would you?"

Without a word, Loretta lifted Raymond's hips, and inserted his penis into her mouth.

"Oh, my God!" Raymond exclaimed. He did not get a sense of hesitation or awkwardness; all he felt was ecstasy. They enjoyed each other for several moments. Raymond's penis grew erect; Loretta struggled to mouth his large organ. As they disengaged, Loretta was gasping for breath, with spit escaping.

Raymond kissed her passionately; she kissed him back. They lay in each other's arms, with Raymond's penis resting outside Loretta's vagina; it softened.

"Put it back in my mouth," Loretta said. Raymond sat on her generous breasts. Because of Loretta's sucking, his penis again hardened; Raymond hurriedly slipped his penis into her vagina; he exploded almost immediately.

"I understand, baby," Loretta said comforting Raymond, "It's been a long time; too long. We still have time left; who knows how much?" They laid in each other's arms, kissing, caressing, expressing their love for each other verbally and physically, being more concerned about the other's feelings than their own. Time passed, but Raymond could not raise an erection no matter how passionate Loretta's actions. He fell asleep.

Two hours later, he awakened; Loretta was asleep. Raymond awakened her by kissing her vagina again. They once again positioned themselves to please each orally. They continued until both orgasmed.

"Do you want another tryst?" asked Raymond.

"No, Babee; I've had enough," Loretta said while breathing heavily.

"Me too."

"We still have time for dinner and a show," said Raymond, after checking his watch while in the bathroom.

"I'd rather just stay here, close to you," Loretta purred.

"Me too."

Raymond and Loretta interlocked bodies while fondling, until both went to sleep.

They awakened early, too early to leave her cabin.

"May I make love to you again?" Raymond asked.

"Of course."

They repeated their rituals; this time Raymond fulfilled her desires with a hard penis. Loretta made a special effort to cause Raymond to orgasm; she got on top, her legs aside his upper body, and rotated. They made love until Raymond climaxed; both were exhausted.

After sleeping another hour or so, Raymond said to Loretta, "That was one of my greatest love-making experiences."

"It was for me, too. I have been loved orally, previously, but never so completely."

"You were both surprising and enjoyable," said Raymond.

"I'll share my secret with you," said Loretta. "Before my first marriage, I had lived a free spirited lifestyle. For several years, while working full-time, I sang with a combo on weekends, and because I had no man in my life, I was the group's girl. My first marriage was at thirty, and it lasted five years. My second was at forty-five, and lasted ten. Neither husband was faithful. I brought into our marriages my earlier, nature, and did not nag, when they could not account for their time away from home. My second husband attempted to 'turn me out'.

"After ending my second marriage, I was very depressed, on occasion, suicidal. A religious friend took me into her church, and helped me restore meaning and worth to my life. But our recent conversations have challenged my perspective."

Saturday morning they were late for breakfast. "Uh huh, uh huh, I know what you two have been up to," teased Camellia.

"Why, whatever do you mean?" Loretta said. Her eyes were fluttering and she was wearing a broad smile. She had a slight crimp in her step. It was difficult, if not impossible, for one woman to hide an intimate, pleasurable night from another woman. Raymond kept his eyes on his plate.

Debarking was almost as complex as embarking. Cabin numbers again, determined the debarking schedule, in groups of fifty. Loretta and Raymond, once again, were separated.

Walter and Raymond shared a cab to Miami's airport and parted emotionally. "See you soon, my brother," Raymond said, while fighting back tears. He then called Loretta while in the airport, with no results.

Several weeks later Raymond called Loretta. "Hey Babee, it's good to hear your voice. When can I come to Tucson?"

"What took you so long? Our religious conversations affected me. I was You inspired me to do some religious research. "I have gained some major insights since returning home."

"What did you learn?"

"Before joining Jesus' entourage, Mary Magdalen was a prostitute. After joining, she had a child. She was pregnant with her second child when Jesus was crucified. No Bible acknowledges her having children, nor who the fathers were, but there is documentation regarding Mary Magdalen's children and their fathers, elsewhere.

"The apostles who wrote the various versions of the bible, believed, or, wanted their readers to believe, that Jesus was a supreme being, without normal sex drives. No one elaborated on the personal relationship between Jesus and Mary Magdalen. I could not find one sentence in any bible that indicated Jesus had a sexual relationship with anyone; he was thirty-four when crucified. That was atypical.

Mary, Jesus' mother, was fifteen when she was impregnated with Jesus; she gave birth at sixteen. Women in Jesus' day became sexually active as early as twelve, yet Jesus reportedly never had a sexual relationship; come on.

"If Jesus is the father of some of Mary Magdalen's children, which is probable, it indicates that Jesus was a normal man, and all of the 'miracles' may have been created by biblical writers.

"I am still active in my church because I enjoy the comradery and the choir; but I no longer contribute as much as I used to, nor do I attend Bible study: thirty-five versions of the Bible, in the Old and New Testaments, is a bit much. Because of our conversations, I no longer look forward to the hereafter. That changes everything.

Damn, thought Raymond, *Loretta is not sounding like the woman on the cruise at all! I am going to cut to the chase.* "Loretta, our last serious conversation involved marriage. Is that still on the table?"

"At the risk of being blunt; no. You were happy to meet me, someone twenty years younger, and I am glad we met. Long range, I need to have someone twenty years younger than myself in my life. We had to work too hard to enjoy ourselves, and that energy level will deteriorate quickly if we marry. Our age variance is too great. As I said earlier, my values, and my needs have changed."

"Once again, when can I come to Tucson?"

"At your convenience, and as I said earlier, you can stay with us. I have vicariously, but completely, introduced you to my sister."

I have no idea what is going to happen when I visit Tucson, but I cannot wait to find out. "Listen, I'll keep in touch and give you sufficient notice."

"Love hearing from you; I can't wait until you visit. I have made my and my sister's reservations for next year's cruise; I hope you and Walter have made yours; they fill-up quickly.

I'll make your visit here and our next cruise memorable; that is unless somebody forty or younger comes along," Loretta said in a deep, whispery voice.

"Hey, buddy," Raymond said to Walter during their next conversation over the phone, "I'm going to Tucson to see Loretta within the next month; are you ready for another cruise?"

#   #   #   #